Helping people find their true identities.

by
Ido Uto-Uko

Box Man

Copyright © 2011 Ido Uto-Uko

ISBN: 978-1-61170-018-3

Inside illustrations by: Ini Uto-Uko
Cover illustration by: Jorge Jimenez

Printed in the United States of America

To purchase additional copies of this book go to:
www.rp–author.com/uto-uko

Robertson Publishing
59 N. Santa Cruz Avenue, Suite B
Los Gatos, California 95030 USA
(888) 354-5957 • www.RobertsonPublishing.com

Dedicated to my mom, Eno Uto-Uko,
who taught me the value of

Learning,
Leadership,
~ and ~
Love.

CHAPTER 1

The Beginning

$$- \quad - \quad - \quad - \quad - \quad - \quad - \quad - \quad - \quad - \quad -$$

It is mid-afternoon and the sky is drenched in red-orange. The end of the summer is here as tree branches bend and leaves are falling. There is a courtship of nature's beauty as court-filled sounds are calling.

A man is placed in the middle of a comfortable park. People are playing three-on-three basketball, reading novels, and enjoying themselves while painting murals and viewing fine urban art.

Unsure and skeptical by the things that are around, his hands are bent, and face placed pointed towards the grassy ground. He is garnished with the garb of classical 21st century hip-hop fashion ware. With ivory sweat pants, boots, a pull-over, head-wrap, and a determined attitude that does not care.

Adorned with a golden shine of a simple bodily force field. His future encounters will make him strong so that one day he can be seen by all, in hopes that he can be healed.

Politely given the name Box, for he is invisible to the unfaithful, for it is they that doubt. Pondering a thought he thinks to himself, "I wish there was a way I can be seen and earn some clout."

Particularly placed by a strongly rooted oak known as the touching tree, he finds an unquenchable strength in its foundation and in its comfort he is happy.

It is at this time he notices a crowd gathered under a gracefully structured white gazebo. People are intensely running around some type of object inside and without knowledge of where to go.

Box Man: "Maybe I should move there? I think I should take a look? Possibly there is a party? For whatever it is-it seems to be off the hook."

The people are reading from a piece of paper. They are looking puzzled at the document, as if they are attempting to solve a mystery caper.

There is a list of famous peoples names that appear: Ludwig Van Beethoven, Albert Einstein, Toni Morrison, and Tupac Shakur.

"What is this I view? What is this I glance? If I go back in time will these great people give me a chance?"

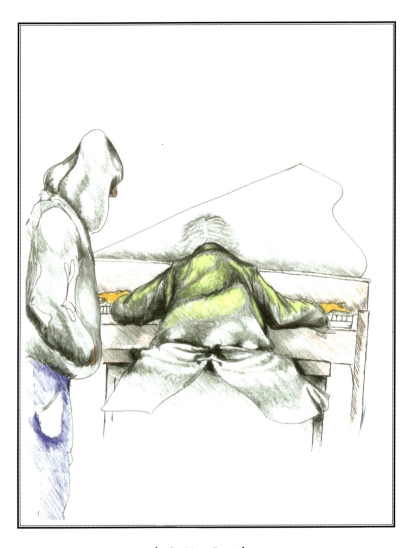

Ludwig Van Beethoven,
December 17, 1770—March 26, 1827

Ludwig Van Beethoven was a German composer and pianist. He is considered to have been one of the most important figures in classical music. Many people today have learned from his music.

Chapter 2

Music Man

— — — — — — — — — — —

Box Man: "I think I'll begin with Beethoven. For they say that music tames the savage beast inside. Maybe if I help him to write great lyrics I can hold my head up with great pride"

Box Man spreads his arms and snaps three times. Beethoven is in a room placing his prints precisely on a petite piano when Box Man appears. Beethoven was given many talents at birth, but still lacks the talent to hear.

The room is filled only with a bed, dresser, and a curled up Beethoven playing his music in the room's oval center. There is a three-second lull of silence as the man enters.

Beethoven acknowledges the man with a bowed head nod and a cordial handshake. The two men smile at one another like a reunion of two old classmates.

Beethoven: "I need your help man. I need your assistance writing this muse. I need your help man or this competition I might lose."

Box Man: "Look. Be focused on that, but just let it flow. There are many things you can call it, but my suggestion is to call it a concerto. Just believe in yourself and have the faith that you can. Understand that the true value locked within your fingertips, for one day you will be a great man."

Beethoven: "Thank you for your wisdom sir. But, for now I must play. I know you have other adventures you must pursue, and for that you cannot stay. Hopefully, you have learned something from me as I have of you. Continue on your journey, young man, and always stay true."

Box man nods his head in agreement. Pauses to cherish the moment and the time spent. He looks down at his left leg and sees the bottom of the golden force field is no longer there.

He does not falter and does not despair. With arms stretched out he snaps his fingers three consecutive times. It comes out like a smooth synchronized musical line.

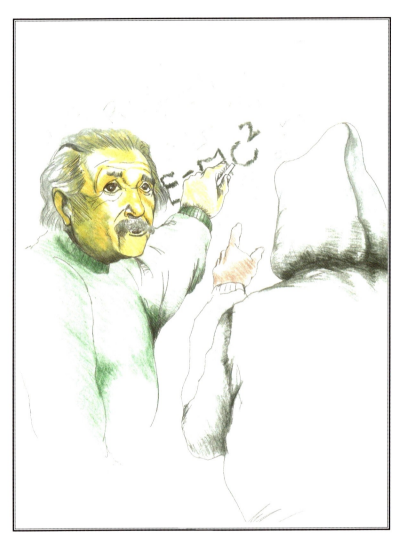

Albert Einstein,
March 14, 1879—April 18, 1955

Albert Einstein was a scientist, philosopher, and teacher. He is considered to be one of the most highly-regarded thinkers of his time. He won the Nobel Prize in physics in 1921. Einstein helped many people during his lifetime, even the president. One of his greatest theories is the theory of relativity.

CHAPTER 3

Bright Idea

— — — — — — — — — — —

The next person he decides to visit is Albert Einstein.

Einstein is very intelligent, but he cannot comb his hair, tie his shoes, or tell the time. He is in his lab with bottles of colorful formula all around. With over fifty patents documented he still writes backward and has trouble getting his thoughts down.

Einstein: His head is looking down at the ground (talking to himself). "This is a shame. This is a pity. I wish I had some help from somebody from another place or city."

Einstein: "What is this I view? What is this I see? Is this my young reflection staring back at me? Maybe I have been in the lab for much to long of a time? Can this be another equation that my dyslexic mind has to climb?"

Box Man: "Don't trip Einstein. Don't even fear. I came to help you solve you equation and that is the true reason I have appeared."

Einstein, (has a smile on his face) "You're right!!! I am working on an equation about why people fuss and fight."

Box Man: "Everybody should learn to make communication work twice. Teach them about relative theories and guide them toward the light."

Einstein: "I got it. A relative theory that would make

(E) equals (M) (C) square. E is equality we must all share. M is for making the foundation that shows people you care. C is for the community of the people that should always be there."

Box Man: (Smiles and reaches in his pocket and throws an object to Einstein.) "Alright, just make sure your hair gets combed."

Box Man stretches his fingers and snaps three more times. He is beginning to understand that a purpose filled life is something that people must all find. He looks down and sees the force field on his right leg is now gone. The man now elects to visit a revolutionary writer and a creator of a California "Love" song.

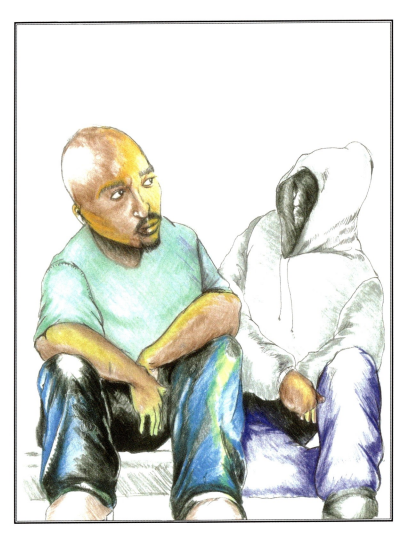

Tupac Shakur
June 16, 1971—September 13, 1996

Tupac Amaru Shakur is best known by his follow-ers as 2Pac. He was a revolutionary musician and writer during the 20th century. He used music as a way to speak out against injustices he felt that was in his community.

CHAPTER 4

Chillin

— — — — — — — — — — —

The person is none other than 20th century musician Tupac Shakur. He is respected because he fought for what is true and pure.

Shakur is found sitting on an oil-stained cement curb. His heart is strong, but for some reason his face looks perturbed. He has a head full of thoughts, a ream of paper, and ideas that he just cannot conform to words.

The setting around him is a twentieth urban dwelling known as a ghetto. There are broken home-windows, babies crying, and young men playing milk crate basketball with dreams of turning pro. Tupac lifts his head to great Box Man. He is dressed in a black T-shirt, sweats, sneakers, and a headband.

"What's up homie?" yells Tupac.

"What's the deal trigger?" states Box Man.

"Chillin. What's up with you?" says Tupac

"Just trying to earn some scrilla," relinquishes Box Man.

Tupac stands up and looks Box Man in the eye. He pauses for a second. Then gives a reply.

Tupac: "Are you somebody I roughed up in my past. Or are you some white suit man hiding behind a hooded mask?"

Box Man: "No dog, I am not a homie from your past whom

you claimed to have roughed. I am just a brother that's here to tell you that you need to keep you head up."

Tupac shrugs, and then sighs at Box Man. He does not believe the hooded figure and thinks he is trying to run a scam.

"I feel you don't believe me because I am fitted in all white. Just think of me as a thug angel that's here to help you with your plight," states a pondering Box Man.

"I hear the words that you're trying to spit. But, I'm tried of people talking about politics and preaching from pulpits. They are talking loud. But, they don't seem to be giving a lick!" yells out Tupac.

"I'm not sweet. But, Pac you are like the rose that grew from concrete," says Box Man as he tries to convince Tupac.

"Say What!!" says a surprised Tupac.

Box Man: "You learned to walk without having feet. Sometimes great things come from nothing. All you have to do is believe."

"Are you getting soft on me smarty?" states an angry Tupac.

"No, I just have to tell you that a man's life should be more than making money, having a good time, and searching for the next party," says Box Man.

"So why don't you let me get my paper and pen so I can write about my life of sin." says Shakur as he looks for something to write with.

Box Man: "Pac—possibly writing about your life may help you. But, more importantly it could help others and teach them how to win."

Box Man snaps his fingers three more times. But before he

leaves he teaches Tupac how to earn wealth from investing a nickel and a dime.

There is no longer a left side of his arm's golden force field. It has vanished because he was honest with others and kept it real. The thing that remains the same is the golden crown still on his head. So with legs down and arms spread he feels lead to visit a worthy wordsmith lady.

Toni Morrison
February 18, 1931—

Toni Morrison was born in Lorain, Ohio. Morrison is a Nobel Prize and Pulitzer Prize-winning American novelist, editor, and professor. She is best known for her novels *The Bluest Eye*, *Song of Solomon*, *Beloved*, *Sula*, and *Tar Baby.*

CHAPTER 5

Sweet Lady

Her head is down as she cries like a baby. Morrison (talking to herself) why don't they pay? Is it because I'm black? Or is it something I lack?

Box Man: "Well neither are solid reasons for you to cry or even fret. You must focus on your strengths. You must let them see your inner beauty and make them forget."

Morrison looks up from her paper-filled disastrous-scattered office desk. She does not know what to think of the strange man or what he might do next. She understands the man is from an unusual place. She pauses briefly and thinks to herself that maybe he is a novel character from her Oakwood bookcase.

Morrison speaks to Box Man: "You may be seated." He pulls up a desk chair. "I still cannot believe it."

"You're a childhood friend from Ohio Lorain," says Morrison

Box Man: "No Ms. Morrison. I came to assist you with your discriminating pain."

"Well it's something no white suit man could ever understand."

"Now who is the one prejudging who? You will not listen to me because I am a white suit man."

"I feel the pain is higher than the eye can see blue. It is

tough to live my life. Its difficult when the only person that believes in you is you. When I was young they called me tar baby."

"That's no way to treat a beautiful lady." rebuttals Box Man.

Morrison stands up, wipes her eyes, and paces back and forth throughout the gold wall papered room. Her hands are stretched up and out, like her day of judgment has come too soon.

"You should have heard what they called my sister Sula. She died before I could talk, so I guess you could say I never really knew her."

"Sounds like what you need is to be loved. Pray for faith and hope to the Lord above." Box Man says enthusiastically. "I have a title that may win. Call your next novel Song of Solomon. It is the shortest chapter in the Bible. Solomon is intelligent, a lover, and was tempted by great trial."

Morrison: "Now I will help you with that golden glow on your head."

Box Man: "It's a nuisance. Its something I dread."

"Well seek truth and you will be lead," believes Morrison

Morrison puts her arms down, looks at Box Man in the chair by her desk. She smiles and makes an attempt to help him with his mess.

"It is up to you to snap your fingers and take flight. You have blessed me on my journey and guided me to write. Now go back to your land or holy place. Go back young man for we all want to see your face."

CHAPTER 6

The View

— — — — — — — — — — —

Box Man is back in the soft serenity of the southern park. People are relaxing reading novels and painting fine art. He is preaching to a circular group of four. We don't know their names but they are snapping their fingers screaming, "Encore!! Encore!!!"

"Out of the night that covers me. Black as the pit from pole to pole. I thank whatever gods may be for my unconquerable soul. Beyond the place of wrath and tears looms, but the horrors of the shade. Yet the menace of the years finds me unafraid. It matters not how straight the gate, with charged punishment the scroll. I am the master of my fate. I am the captain of my soul."

CHAPTER 7

The Wrap

— — — — — — — — — — —

We now see the face of the members of the crowd. They're shaking their fingers at Box Man and screaming out loud.

"Unveil your identity. Tell us you true self." states Einstein.

"Are you a rich man?" interjects Beethoven.

"If so dog, then spread the wealth!!" hollers Tupac.

"Maybe you're that bird I released to the Ohio sky. Whatever it is young man, just tell us why," states Morrison.

"Why must you all fuss? Why must you all fight? I have come to show you your fears and make sure everything is all right."

Box Man takes off his hood and begins to unravel his wrap. With arms spread he does his usual three-finger circle snap. There is a seven-second pause and screams of amaze. For the only thing left is a white suit and a mirror that now lay.

LaVergne, TN USA
08 March 2011
219302LV00001BA